# THE TECHNOLOGY OF ANCIENT EGYPT

M. Solodky

rosen central™

The Rosen Publishing Group, Inc., New York

*To Alice*

Published in 2006 by The Rosen Publishing Group, Inc.
29 East 21st Street, New York, NY 10010

Copyright © 2006 by The Rosen Publishing Group, Inc.

First Edition

**Library of Congress Cataloging-in-Publication Data**

Solodky, M.
The technology of ancient Egypt/M. Solodky.
   p. cm.—(The technology of the ancient world)
Includes bibliographical references.
ISBN 1-4042-0557-8 (library binding)
1. Technology—Egypt—History—To 1500—Juvenile literature. 2. Egypt—Civilization—
To 332 B.C.—Juvenile literature. I. Title. II. Series.

T27.3.E3S65 2005
609.32—dc22

                        2005010750

*Manufactured in the United States of America*

**On the cover**: The background shows brick-making and smelting workmen who are featured on a wall painting from the Eighteenth Dynasty (sixteenth–fourteenth centuries BC). It is from the Tombs of the Nobles in Thebes, Egypt. The photo inset shows a figure of a man with a hoe, dating from the Sixth Dynasty (circa 2250 BC) in Assiut, Egypt.

# CONTENTS

# INTRODUCTION

# LIFE ALONG
# THE NILE

Egyptian civilization never would have existed had it not been for the Nile River. When the first peoples settled in Egypt, the world's longest river—which flows from its sources in Ethiopia and Uganda to the Mediterranean Sea—was lined with lush valleys. The valleys provided a green oasis amid a desert region with little rainfall. Each year, the river flooded, irrigating the surrounding plains. When the waters receded, they left behind deposits of black silt that were rich with vitamins and minerals.

Ancient Egyptians regarded the flood as a miracle. They built one of the world's great civilizations along the river's fertile shores. The Nile offered Egyptians many resources and riches. In countless ways, the river also shaped the inventions, activities, and technologies developed by the people whose lives depended upon it. Its waters were channeled into irrigation systems that permitted large-scale cultivation. Aside from providing Egyptians with food, the Nile also played a significant role in the invention of the world's first paper, which was made from papyrus plants that grew along its banks. It also supplied an essential means of transportation. Via the great river, thousands of workers hauled the ten-ton (nine-metric-ton) stones that were used to make the immense pyramids. And these marvels of architectural and engineering technology remain impressive.

A majestic view of the great pyramids of Egypt is seen here through a row of elegant palm trees. The pyramids are proof of one among many of the creative, imaginative, and skilled technological innovations for which ancient Egyptians are admired.

This is a fine example of a classic mid-nineteenth century decorative map of Egypt and Arabia Petrea. Maps of this era were generally very artistic. An illustrated atlas from the period would try to convey the native culture of each country through illustrations placed carefully around each map. An example of this is the trading ships drawn onto the Red Sea to the right and the illustration of the Mosque of Sultan Hassan to the left.

Technology involves combining knowledge and techniques to create a method that allows people to perform a practical task. Egyptians advanced technology in many ways. Their innovations touched on every important aspect of daily life, from hunting, harvesting, and mining, to writing, decorating, and telling time. The tools and techniques they invented were copied and adapted by many future civilizations. In fact, a surprising number of these inventions are still with us today.

# FERTILITY AND FOOD

The first Egyptians who settled along the Nile's banks were farmers. Upon this rich, sacred "black earth," they constructed villages. Beyond the Nile Valley were the hot sands of the Sahara. The ancient Egyptians called the desert the "red earth." They feared the hot desert winds whose clouds of sand and dust could blind humans and animals and destroy crops.

The Nile floods usually occurred between July and September. Sometimes, the high waters came late. Other times, they didn't come at all. Unable to depend on the floods, farmers decided to take matters into their own hands. As early as 5000 BC, ancient Egyptians created the world's first irrigation systems. They began by digging canals that would direct the Nile's waters to distant fields and highlands.

Pictured above is a painted limestone detail of sailors on a boat in the Nile River in Egypt. This image, featuring hieroglyphics on the upper right and left-hand sides, was a decoration on the tomb of Senefer, the mayor of Thebes. The waters that the ancient Egyptians redirected from the Nile River were vital to growing crops.

Later, around 2400 BC, they constructed reservoirs so they could save water for use during dry periods. The world's first reservoir was built at Fayum, Egypt, a desert region. Flooding turned Fayum into a lake. More than twenty miles (thirty-two kilometers) of dikes were built leading from Fayum to the surrounding countryside. This included a canal to the Nile. When the dikes' gates were opened, water flowed through the canals and into dry fields.

Closing the gates trapped the water in the fields where it would evaporate. The moist, fertilized soil left behind would then be perfect for planting.

## Cultivation

Ancient Egyptians raised many types of plants. Grains such as wheat and barley were important crops. Vegetables and herbs were also grown. These included leeks, radishes, cucumbers, peas, beans, asparagus, onions, garlic,

# THE SHADOOF

Farmers also invented a device called a shadoof that was used to bring canal water to the fields. The shadoof was a long pole balanced on a horizontal wooden beam. At one end of the pole was a weight and on the other was a bucket. Pressing down on the weight raised a bucket full of water that could be used for irrigation or drinking. Shadoofs are still common in Egypt.

*A man is using a shadoof to draw water from the Nile. Aside from the ancient Egyptians, the Sumerians of Mesopotamia used a similar system to get water from the Tigris-Euphrates.*

and various spices. Medicinal drugs and dyes were made from certain plants and herbs. The wicker fibers of some plants were woven into mats, baskets, and sandals. Cotton was Egypt's number-one export. Various trees, such as palms and lemon trees, were prized for the shade they provided, the fruits they bore, and the wood they supplied for tools, roof beams, and furniture.

Farmers prepared the earth for planting by tilling it. For this, a hoe was used to loosen the soil. Hoes were made of a thin, sharp-edged blade of hard wood bound to a long wooden shaft with plant-fiber cord. Tilling was followed by plowing. A long blade of hard wood was fastened to two wooden stilts and dragged through the soil by four strong men. Some historians believe that Egyptians were the first people to use plows. Around 2000 BC, cattle took over this back-breaking work.

During planting season (three a year depending on the floods of the Nile), Egyptian farmers had a lot of work. In this wall painting, peasants are using tools to break the ground, sow the land, and plow it in preparation for planting crops such as wheat and barley. Other important crops included vegetables, figs, flax (used to make linen), and vines.

At harvest time, farmers used straight or slightly curved wooden sickles with sharp blades to cut stalks of corn and wheat. Eventually, these tools were redesigned with copper, and then bronze. Axes made from ground-up stone fastened to wooden handles were used to cut wood. Other common tools included wooden shovels, pitchforks, and rakes. Harvested grains were transported in nets and sacks made from leather or canvas.

## Domestic Animals

Ancient Egyptians relied on domestic animals—cattle, sheep, goats, and donkeys—to help them with work. These animals also provided them with meat, milk, wool, and leather. Also, Egyptians raised geese, ducks, and chickens. At specialized farms, chickens were raised. Farmers buried eggs in dunghills, which produced sufficient heat for chicks to hatch.

Egyptians made many attempts to tame wild animals. Pigs were domesticated versions of hairy wild boars. Donkeys, popular beasts of burden—particularly for fieldwork and the transportation of goods and people—were descendants of the Nubian wild ass. Later, between 1000 and 500 BC, Egyptians began to use camels. Camels were better than donkeys for long desert treks. During the hot summer months, camels only needed to drink water once a week.

Horses were initially introduced to Egypt (circa 1500 BC) as a result of wars against Asian kingdoms, whose troops traveled on horseback. In Egypt, only kings and nobles bred horses. Harnessed to light, two-wheeled chariots, the steeds were used for ceremonies, hunts, and military campaigns.

Egyptians were less successful in their attempts to tame the oryx, a straight-hooved antelope. The oryx was one of many wild animals the Egyptians hoped to domesticate. Some pharaohs captured hyenas and even cheetahs to be used as hunting animals. Tame monkeys were popular companions for the nobility, as were domesticated deer and gazelles.

Of course, the animal that Egyptians are most famous for domesticating is the cat. It took thousands of years to tame the North African wildcat into becoming the household feline who kept rats from Egyptian homes and granaries.

## Wild Animals

Before animal breeding became widespread, Egyptians hunted wild animals for their meat and skins. Before the Egyptian state was established and

**In ancient Egypt, cats were highly respected. They were very useful in terms of keeping away mice and other rodents. Sometimes known as "the keepers of the grain," these cats were worshipped to the extent that temples and statues were built in the form of lions, the closest relative to the cat.**

the Nile Delta's marshes were drained, there was an abundance of wild game in Egypt, including giraffes, elephants, rhinoceroses, and gazelles. Later, with the cultivation of the Nile Valley, most large animals disappeared. In the meantime, villagers could depend on their crops and livestock for food.

Hunting weapons included spears, bows and arrows, a type of boomerang, and heavy wooden clubs that were thrown at prey. Peasants usually went after small fowl on foot. However, hunting large animals became a popular sport for kings and nobles. Riding horse-drawn chariots, they proved their bravery by bringing home wild beasts ranging from antelopes and ostriches to more dangerous lions, cheetahs, and leopards.

## Fishing

Breeding animals and hunting large game were difficult for Egyptian peasants. Even with complex irrigation systems in place, there was a limit to the number of pastures that could supply livestock with food. Meat was expensive for poorer Egyptians. Aside from cereals and vegetables, they relied on fish from the river for food. Fishermen used nets, traps, and spear-like harpoons to catch Nile perch, eel, and catfish. In later times, they used rods and lines. Hooks were made from bone, and then from metal.

# THE WRITTEN WORD

Egyptians are often referred to as the inventors of writing. In truth, it isn't clear whether the Egyptians invented writing themselves or if they learned it from their neighbors, the Sumerians. However, historians believe that both peoples began writing around the same time—3100 BC.

The ancient system of Egyptian writing is called hieroglyphics. It was quite different from the Sumerian script, known as cuneiform. Almost all Egyptian writing samples that have survived to this day were discovered by archaeologists in ancient burial tombs.

## Hieroglyphics

The word "hieroglyphic" is Greek for "sacred carving." When the ancient Greeks first arrived in Egypt, they saw hieroglyphs carved on tombs and temple walls. Hieroglyphs were symbols that represented everyday objects. For instance, a picture of a mouth meant "to speak." Over time, new signs were created that represented certain sounds. Placed together with other signs, they would spell out a word. Number hieroglyphs were also developed to calculate mathematical problems. This was important for accounting.

**These hieroglyphics were dedicated to an Egyptian fertility god. Generally, the Egyptians wrote from top to bottom. To read hieroglyphics, one needs first to identify the symbols whose front and back are an obvious, such as the birds above. The bird is facing the beginning of the text.**

Egyptians' use of written hieroglyphs was revolutionary. It set them apart from all other oral societies that communicated by word of mouth, and it paved the way for the development of other written languages.

Over time, hieroglyphs were replaced by a script called hieratic, which was invented around 2800 BC. Though the Egyptians continued to use hieroglyphs to decorate religious monuments, they wrote documents in hieratic. Hieratic was easier to compose. Around 600 BC, a more practical script called demotic was brought into use. Its characters, similar to modern Western script, could be written more quickly.

In all, more than 700 different hieroglyphs were in use. The difficulty of learning so many signs partially explains why only 1 percent of the population could read or write. In general, only the sons of wealthy Egyptians learned how to do so. Many became professional scribes (writers), which was considered to be a very important social position. Even early rulers could not write or read. They relied on scribes to read and write messages and important documents. Young scribes had to study for years at

These scribal palates—ink wells *(bottom)* and brushes *(top)*—were the tools employed by scribes. In Egyptian society, scribes were treated with enormous respect. For example, they never had to do physical labor and they never went hungry. It is because of their writing skills that knowledge of ancient Egyptian customs is known today.

special schools. Some began their training at age ten.

## Scribes

The scribe's main tool was called a kalamos. This pen was made from a six-inch (fifteen-centimeter) reed. Its ends were chewed by scribes to form a brushlike tip. Pens of different sizes were used depending on the thickness and color of the script. Ultimately, a scribe's job was more similar to drawing or painting than to writing. Accordingly, ancient scribes used a variety of colored inks made from plants and minerals. Documents were later written only in black or red.

Ancient scribes wrote while standing or kneeling. It wasn't until after 2000 BC that they began to use desks. Scribes often worked together under the watchful eye of a chief scribe. Often the chief scribe dictated a message,

This sculpture shows how papyrus scrolls were made. The reeds of the papyrus plant were flattened and then pounded into a long sheet. Paper made from papyrus was so strong and lightweight that a better method was not developed until the Arabs started using paper made from pulp. As a result, the papyrus plant was no longer cultivated and died out in Egypt.

which could then be copied by various writers at the same time.

## Papyrus

Although the earliest hieroglyphs were cut into stone monuments or inscribed onto clay tablets, both surfaces were hard to write on, heavy to transport, and difficult to store. It was hardly a coincidence that the first examples of paper, called papyrus, date from 3000 BC, the time when

Egyptians began to write. The invention of papyrus transformed Egyptian society and revolutionized the way people kept valuable information.

Papyrus, made from the papyrus plant, is a triangular-shaped reed that used to grow in abundance along the banks of the Nile. In Egyptian, "papyrus" means "property of Pharaoh." In fact, the pharaohs—for whom written records and documents were essential—carefully controlled the production of papyrus. Ancient Greeks used Egyptian papyrus, which they called *papure*. This, in turn, became the English word "paper."

## Making Scrolls

Papyrus was made by tearing off the reed's outer "skin." After soaking the reeds in water, the Egyptians placed these thin strips in layers on top of each other. They were hammered into a single flat sheet and then left to dry in the sun. Finally, the papyrus was stretched and then pressed smooth by being placed between heavy stones for several days.

In general, papyrus surfaces were cut to a standard size: about 8.5 inches (22 cm) in width and up to 16 inches (41 cm) in length. Twenty such "pages" added together made up a papyrus scroll. Although an average scroll was 14.75 feet (4.5 m) long, scrolls have been found that measure up to 30 feet (9 m).

Since the Nile region was the major source of papyrus, ancient Egyptians controlled the manufacture and sale of papyrus for centuries. Foreigners tried very hard to discover the carefully guarded recipe for this high-quality (and expensive) paper, but the technology was a carefully guarded secret. As a result, other countries sought out alternatives. This, in turn, led to the invention (circa 150 BC) of parchment, the precursor of the paper we use today.

# MEANS OF MEASUREMENT

Ancient Egypt was one of the richest civilizations of the pre-Christian world. To keep track of and maintain such wealth, the Egyptians developed many techniques of measuring and record keeping.

## Bookkeeping

Scribes kept detailed inventories, drew up contracts, and kept thorough records of all economic activities. They noted everything: the amount of seeds planted and the number of bags of grain harvested, the types and quantities of objects manufactured by craftspeople, and the building supplies used on construction sites. Scribes also accompanied military campaigns and took detailed notes of treasures seized from foreign powers. They created lists of objects and animals that were sacrificed to the gods.

These records, which were written on everything from papyrus to pieces of broken pottery (for quick business receipts), allowed the Egyptian government to keep a detailed account of its wealth. Ultimately, this refined technology led to the advancement of Egyptian culture. With such information, officials could plan for special projects and distribute goods to those in need.

## Telling Time

Running an organized society also meant keeping track of time. Ancient Egyptians developed two important ways of doing this: clocks and calendars.

### Clocks

To tell time, Egyptians relied on water clocks and sundials. A water clock functioned like an hourglass. Instead of sand, a container full of water dripped through a tiny hole into a second container placed beneath it. Both containers had marks carved into their sides. When the water had dropped from one mark to the next, it meant that an hour had gone by. The only problem with this invention was that somebody had to refill it constantly.

The interior of this reproduction of an ancient Egyptian water clock is marked with ten columns of twelve indentations. After filling the clock with water, it would seep through the holes in the sides, from top to bottom. Though this invention was an ingenious way to measure the passage of time, it was not very accurate. Nonetheless, water clocks were one of the earliest recorded methods of telling the time that did not rely upon observing the planets.

The sundial, a circle with marks or numbers written around its edges, is not unlike modern clocks. A little stick that functioned as an hour hand was fastened to the middle of the circle. As

# STUDYING THE STARS

Ancient Egyptians depended on the stars to help them measure time and directions. Certain stars called decans allowed them to calculate the time at night. Studying the positions of certain stars also helped Egyptians locate north, south, east, and west.

the sun moved through the sky, the stick's shadow fell on different numbers. The only problem with the sundial was that it couldn't be used at night.

## The Egyptian Calendar

The ancient Egyptians were the inventors of the 365-day calendar, which is similar to the one commonly used in the West today. Egyptians divided the year into three seasons. The first season, Akhet, marked the beginning of the floods and lasted from July to October. The second season, Proyet, coincided with the growth of crops and spanned from November to February. The last season,

Shomu, marked the start of the harvest season. It lasted from March to June. Each month was three weeks; one week consisted of ten days. Added to the beginning of the year were five holy days. This added up to a 365-day calendar—the very first one in history.

Egyptians used written calendars. Days of each month were written down in black ink—a reminder of the fertile black land from which so much life sprung. Days that were considered unlucky were marked on calendars in red. Red was a reminder of the dry red desert, which symbolized danger and destruction.

# GREAT CONSTRUCTIONS

Ancient Egypt was ruled by powerful kings called pharaohs. The pharaohs owned all lands, created all laws, and controlled the army. Considered divine beings with links to the Egyptian gods, pharaohs were the highest religious leaders in the land. They led important religious ceremonies and constructed great temples to honor Egypt's many gods and goddesses.

## The Great Pyramids

It is impossible to think about Egypt without thinking about the great pyramids that rise up out of its sands. Pyramids were built as magnificent tombs for the pharaohs. Known as "houses of eternity"— in which the pharaoh, his wives, children, slaves, and even pets would be entombed together—these pyramids were quite grand.

The pyramids at Giza were an immense undertaking of architectural innovation and skill. In the first stages of production, the site was cleared. Next, large blocks of stone were transported and put into place. It is not known exactly how these gigantic, heavy stones were positioned, but one theory is that levers were used to help lift the blocks.

The first pyramid was built for pharaoh Djoser circa 2650 BC by architect Imhotep. It is known as the Step Pyramid because it resembles an enormous staircase. Egyptians believed that after climbing the stairs, pharaohs would meet the sun god in the sky. Other pharaohs built Step Pyramids. Aside from Djoser's, none of them has survived.

It wasn't until around 2600 BC that pharaoh Snefru built the first pyramid with smooth, sloping sides. This shape represented the original landmass that, according to Egyptian religion, rose out of the waters at the beginning of time. In 2589 BC, pharaoh Khufu ordered the construction of the impressive Great Pyramid at Giza. Considered one of the Seven Wonders of the Ancient World, it took some twenty years to complete. More than two million blocks of limestone—weighing between 2.5 and 15 tons (2.3 and 13.6 m tons)—were used to build it. At 450 feet (137 m), the Great Pyramid stands taller than New York's Statue of Liberty.

## How to Build a Pyramid

Building a pyramid was an enormous undertaking that involved thousands of men and years of work. Modern architects and engineers still marvel at the innovative technology the Egyptians employed. After marking the pyramid's dimensions in the sand, workers began cutting giant blocks of stone from nearby quarries. Ancient Egyptians didn't have machines to crush and cut rocks for their buildings and sculptures. Instead, they relied on their own strength and a few useful tools.

Most pyramids were made from limestone found in the hills near the east bank of the Nile. Workers either cut blocks from the surface rock or tunneled into the hillside to extract what they needed. They cut the limestone with saws and chisels made of copper and, later, bronze. Wedges were then used to detach the block of rock from its base so it could be transported.

Modern scholars continue to be amazed by the immense physical force required to move the enormously heavy blocks from the mines onto the large barges that carried them down the Nile. From the barges, the stones were dragged onto sleds that were pushed and pulled to the building site. Water was poured into the sand to smooth the way for the sled. Workers and craftsmen labored year-round on these great construction projects. During the flood season, the pharaoh summoned field workers and farmers to help.

At the pyramid site, it was easy to arrange the blocks on the ground level. It was more challenging to construct the upper layers of the pyramid. Workers built ramps of mud bricks, limestone chips, and clay to hoist these multi-ton blocks up from the ground. After dragging or pushing the blocks up the ramps, they set them into place on the next level. As the pyramid got bigger, the ramps grew higher and their bases became wider. Various ramps were erected on each of the pyramids' four sides. The pyramids were so well constructed that more than eighty still exist. Aside from a few chipped blocks, many show little damage. The blocks fit together so tightly that one cannot even stick a razor blade in the space between them.

When the Great Pyramid was almost completed, a special block covered in glittery metal (gold or electrum) was

## "KING TUT"

For a long time, Egyptologists (experts who specialize in the study of ancient Egyptian culture) believed that all of the pharaohs' buried treasures had been looted by thieves. Then, in 1922, American archaeologist Howard Carter came upon an undiscovered tomb in the Valley of the Kings. It belonged to the young pharaoh Tutankhamen (reigned 1333–1323 BC). Tutankhamen became pharaoh at the age of nine and died at nineteen. Miraculously, almost all the objects buried with the young prince were still in the tomb. They included clothes, jewelry, weapons, furniture, and model boats—many of which were made of pure gold or decorated in gold leaf. Today, these treasures are housed at the Cairo Museum and in Tutankhamen's tomb in the Valley of the Kings.

*There are mainly two theories about the cause of Tutankhamen's death: his delicate health, or murder because of his interest in politics.*

placed at the top. The outer layer of the entire pyramid was covered in white limestone to make its edges shiny and smooth. Pyramids rarely stood alone. They were often part of vast complexes that included smaller pyramids for pharaohs' wives and temples reserved for offerings.

Pharaohs were laid to rest deep inside the pyramids in special burial chambers. Thick granite doors and false passages made it difficult for robbers to enter these rooms and steal the riches buried with the pharaohs. Despite such care, historians believe that by 1000 BC all the pyramids had been looted.

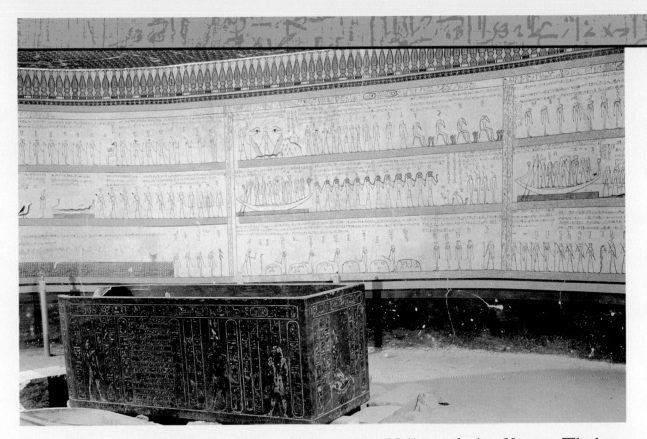

This is the interior of a tomb in the Valley of the Kings, Thebes. Because the tomb is small, archaeologists believed that the ancient Egyptians were short. The wall painting behind the coffin illustrates the journey to the afterlife. It was believed that such lavish decoration would ensure that those buried were well received in the next world.

## Tombs and Temples

Between 1500 and 1000 BC, almost all pharaohs were buried in ornate tombs in the Valley of the Kings. Some tombs were placed high up among the valley's steep hillsides where their entrances would be almost invisible to robbers. Others boasted highly decorated doors that called attention to their wealthy occupants.

Most tombs had long corridors leading to chambers where the pharaohs were laid to rest with their wealth and possessions. Even though many entrances were guarded, thieves eventually succeeded in robbing almost all of these tombs of their precious belongings.

Religious temples were built of stone so they would last forever. These important buildings were considered homes for gods and goddesses when

25

Pharaoh Ramses II had two temples built into an immense rocky cliff in 1257 BC. Abu Simbel used to be known as the land of Nubia. Even before Ramses, this part of the landscape had been sacred. Ramses dedicated the temple to the sun gods Amon-Re and Re-Horakhte.

they visited Earth. Ancient Egyptians believed in hundreds of different gods, many of whom were associated with specific animals. The most important god of all was the sun god, who was considered the creator of all life.

Gods and goddesses were worshipped by pharaohs and priests, who lived in the temples and laid out offerings of food and drink for the gods. Temple walls were decorated with carved scenes and painted with bright colors. Most temples featured stone sculptures of the gods and goddesses in whose honor they were built. One of the most famous is at Abu Simbel in southern Egypt. There, the pharaoh Ramses II ordered two temples to be carved into the sandstone cliffs. At the entrance, two gigantic statues of the pharaoh himself soar to a height of 69 feet (21 m).

## Egyptian Homes

Egyptian houses were quite sophisticated. They were built out of mud bricks. Mud was gathered from the banks of the Nile and carried to the construction site in leather buckets. Workers added straw and pebbles to the mud to make it stronger before pouring it into wooden frames. Left in the sun, the mud hardened into bricks.

Once the bricks had been laid, the walls were covered in plaster made from limestone. Often decorated with geometric designs or scenes from nature, they were painted in lively colors. Small windows kept out dust and sunlight while air vents allowed air to circulate. Decorative clay tiles kept the floors cool. Aristocratic families had large mansions with many rooms and stairs that led to breezy rooftops. Their gardens often featured swimming pools in which lotus flowers grew and fish swam. Wealthier homes were furnished with handmade wooden furniture ranging from stools and beds to ornately decorated boxes and storage chests. Carved headrests, used instead of pillows, supported sleepers' necks and kept their heads away from poisonous insects and scorpions that crept across the floor. The techniques employed by Egyptian builders provided homes that were extremely comfortable, even by today's standards.

# MUMMIES AND MEDICINE

Some of the most skilled medical practitioners of the ancient world were Egyptians. They knew a considerable amount about the human body and the diseases that could affect it. Over centuries, Egyptian knowledge and technology helped develop many medicines and surgical procedures.

## Anatomy

Ancient Egyptians were quite familiar with human anatomy and with how internal organs, such as livers and lungs, functioned. Much of their knowledge came from studying animals that were regularly butchered and cooked. They also learned a lot from the process of embalming and mummifying their dead.

## Mummification

The first peoples who settled in Egypt buried their dead in shallow holes in the desert. The heat and dryness of the sand dehydrated the bodies quickly, preventing them from rotting and keeping them astonishingly lifelike. Over time, however, Egyptians began placing corpses in coffins to prevent them from being dug up and eaten by wild animals. However, without the hot, dry desert sands to preserve them, corpses soon rotted. This was a problem because ancient Egyptians believed in an eternal afterlife in which a person would require the use of his or her body. As a result, Egyptians developed a technique of preserving bodies so they would remain as lifelike as possible. Today, this technique is known as mummification.

Mummification was a fairly complicated process. After death, a body was first taken to a purifying temple where embalmers washed it with fragrant palm wine and water from the Nile. Once cleansed, a cut was made in the left side of the body through which all internal organs were removed. A long hook was used to smash the brain and

This mummy *cartonnage*, a highly decorative coffin dating from circa 945–653 BC, is made of a mixture of linen or papyrus and plaster. It contains the preserved body of Nespanetjerepenere, a well-respected priest in ancient Egypt. The coffin is beautifully painted and inlaid with glass and jewels such as lapis lazuli (a precious blue stone).

29

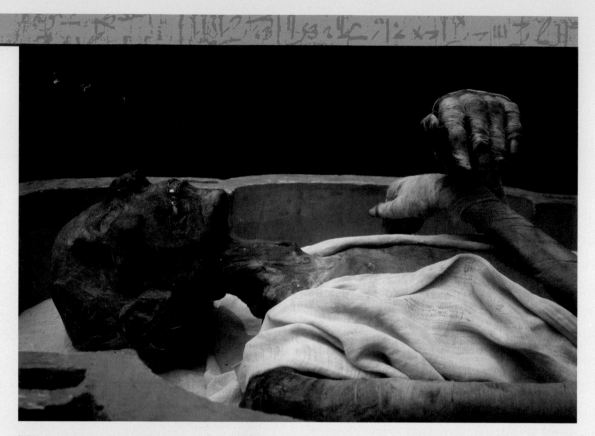

The mummy of Ramses II is one of the best-preserved mummies found by archaeologists. In the 1970s, the mummy was examined with x-rays, and it was discovered that the Pharaoh's nose had been stuffed with peppercorns. That is what kept its distinctive shape. Most noses of mummies were flattened with layers of bandages.

pull it out through the nose. These organs were removed because they rotted quickly. The liver, lungs, stomach, and intestines were all washed and packed in natron to dry them out. Natron was a crystal substance made of sodium carbonate and sodium bicarbonate that kept bodies dried and well preserved. Only the heart remained in the body. Egyptians believed this essential organ was responsible for all human thoughts and feelings, as well as for the body's functioning as a whole.

With the organs removed, the body was stuffed with natron, dry leaves, and sawdust, then left to dry out. After forty days, the body was once again washed with water from the Nile and then rubbed with sweet-smelling oils to keep the skin smooth and elastic. Dehydrated organs were wrapped in linen and replaced inside the body or sealed in special containers

These canopic jars feature decorative wooden lids that represent the Sons of Horus, four minor gods who were responsible for protecting the human organs of the mummies that were placed inside them. From left to right, the jars contain intestines, a stomach, lungs, and a liver.

called canopic jars. These stone or wooden jars were often buried alongside the mummy.

Once the embalming was completed, the oiled and cleansed body was wrapped in strips of fine linen. Workers glued the strips together with a liquid resin. The completely bandaged body, or mummy, was wrapped in a cloth decorated with a painted portrait of Osiris, god of the underworld. The mummy was then laid in a coffin, which was placed in another coffin. Some of these coffins, especially those belonging to princes and pharaohs, were beautiful works of art that were ornately painted and covered with gold.

## Diseases and Cures

Many of the specialists involved in mummification became experts at performing autopsies. An autopsy is an examination of a body to discover

## SOME COMMON CURES

Some of the herbs and minerals used as remedies by ancient Egyptians (such as garlic and yeast) are still used today. Others are less popular.

### For Diarrhea:
Bread dough, corn, fresh earth, onion, 1/8th cup figs and grapes, and elderberry.

### For Skin Lesions:
Once the scab falls off, apply a mixture of scribe's excrement and fresh milk.

### For Burns:
Apply a mixture of gum, ram's hair, and milk from a woman who has borne a male child.

### For Indigestion:
Crush a hog's tooth and place the powder in four sugar cakes. Eat a cake each day for four days.

### For Cataracts:
Mix the brain of a tortoise with honey. Place it on the eye while reciting a prayer.

the cause of death. Through autopsies, ancient Egyptians developed considerable knowledge about common ailments and diseases. Many of their findings were written down on papyrus scrolls and studied by generations of doctors who compiled a list of more than 200 illnesses. Medical scholars consider them to be the first advanced medical texts in the world.

More than just physicians' manuals, these texts protected doctors against possible medical error. By following the texts' instructions, doctors would not be charged with malpractice if their patients died. However, if it was proved they did not follow proper procedure, doctors could be put to death for criminal negligence.

There were many kinds of doctors in ancient Egypt, ranging from eye doctors and head doctors to stomach specialists and dentists. Egyptian surgeons were among the first physicians in the world to set broken bones and to use anesthestics in surgery. They also practiced reconstructive surgery using artificial noses and ears to replace damaged ones.

Egyptian doctors were fairly accurate at identifying and curing surface wounds such as cuts, burns, swelling, and fractures. However, diseases caused by internal organs, such as the lungs and liver, were a mystery to them. They believed bad luck or evil spirits caused such illnesses. As a cure, they often combined prayers and good luck charms with remedies made from plant, mineral, or animal sources.

# CHEMISTS AND CRAFTSMEN

**A**ncient Egyptians were extraordinarily skilled artists and craftsmen. They developed advanced techniques and tools for working with stone, wood, metal, glass, and fabrics. These techniques allowed them to create objects that were both functional and beautiful.

## Metals

The mining of precious metals was an important activity. Thousands of Egyptians worked in mines and quarries. These were owned by the pharaohs and managed by their sons or most trusted nobles. Ancient Egyptians used sophisticated methods to mine and extract metals. They also developed techniques of melting and mixing them to create new metals—called alloys—which were very strong, flexible, and very attractive. As a result of their expertise

A tomb painting of a jewelry-making workshop illustrates the specialized metal tools that the Egyptians had developed to aid craftsmen in creating specialized and intricate art, sculpture, decorations, and jewelry. For example, the craftsman on the right is holding in a piece of copper in a brazier while using a blowpipe to increase the heat.

with metals, Egyptians also acquired an advanced knowledge of chemistry (the science of substances, their characteristics, and the transformations they undergo).

As early as 3400 BC, copper was a commonly employed metal. It was used to make tools that included everything from needles, drill bits, and chisels to saws, axes, and adzes (a carpenter's tool used to smooth the rough edges of wooden objects).

Bronze, an alloy of copper and tin, produced sharp cutting blades for knives, swords, and razors. Most weapons were also made from bronze. These included daggers, battle-axes, spears, and arrowheads. By 800 BC, iron (a foreign import) had become more commonly used than copper. Egyptians called iron "the metal of heaven," perhaps because early samples came from meteorites that had fallen to Earth.

# GOLDEN RECIPES

Egyptians were famous alchemists. Alchemy was the ancient science of transforming metals into gold. Instruction manuals for manufacturing gold and other precious metals such as electrum (a mixture of gold and silver) were written on papyri. There were directions for testing the purity of gold and for making artificial gold, gold leaf, and even gold ink for writing. There were also laboratory recipes for making alloys, soldering metals, and coloring metallic surfaces. These recipes were guarded as secrets by pharaohs and their chemists. However, some pharaohs lived in fear that these valuable techniques would fall into greedy enemy hands. As such, in AD 290, Roman emperor Diocletian (who ruled Egypt at the time) passed a law calling for the destruction of all alchemical recipes. The only texts that survived were several papyri buried in the tombs of Egyptian chemists.

*Found during an archaeological dig, this intricate and beautifully detailed necklace features the likeness of a falcon. Known as a vulture collar, this piece dates from circa 945–925 BC. In 1999, archaeologists found a 2,900-year-old papyrus map that lead them to approximately 16 million dollars in pure gold.*

## Gold

The Egyptian pharaohs were famous and much envied for the vast quantities of gold they possessed. Using fires and furnaces, goldsmiths and artists melted this precious metal and molded or hammered it into stunning statues, mummy masks, and jewelry. Many of Egypt's gold mines were located in a region known as Nubia, or "land of gold."

Egyptians mined for gold in caves and cliffs as well as in rivers. To discover the gold in rivers, miners piled bedrock sand into a woolen bag with a fleecy interior. After adding water, the bag was shaken by two men. When the water and sand were poured out, the heavier particles of gold would be stuck to the fleece.

## Glassmaking

Most historians agree that glass is an Egyptian invention. Even before the pharaohs ruled Egypt, glass objects—primarily jars, figures, and glass-beaded jewelry—were being produced in large quantities. Early potters discovered it when they fired clay vessels. The sand and metal fragments in the clay melted together to produce glass.

Initially, glass was shaped using clay molds that were baked in furnaces or ovens. In later times, glass was blown using long reeds with clay tips.

Egyptian artists fashioned exquisite jewelry out of colorful glass beads. Although many legends tell of wealthy Egyptians who wore enormous rubies and emeralds, most of these jewels were actually well-made fakes that were manufactured from glass. Egyptian jewelers were also renowned for false pearls, which were exported throughout the world.

## Textiles and Clothing

One of the oldest fabrics made by humans is linen. Archaeologists discovered samples of linen cloth in Egypt that date from 5000 BC. Linen was made from flax, a plant that Egyptians grew in fields along the banks of the Nile. After being harvested, the flax plants were dried, combed, soaked in water, and then beaten to separate the fibers from the plants' woody core. The fibers were twisted together and then spun into thread on sticks or spindles. Using looms, threads were woven into fabric. Using knives and scissors of copper and bronze, seamstresses

# MAKING PEARLS

Artificial pearls were made from a type of quartz crystal. The quartz was soaked in a mixture of powdered alum (a type of stone that contained aluminum, potassium, and sulfate) and mixed with the urine of a young boy. It was then placed in a clay vessel containing "quicksilver" (a silvery, pearly mineral also known as mercury) and fresh milk from a woman's breast that was heated over a fire.

To make the artificial pearls white and shiny, several methods were used. One was to dip them in a boiled mixture of water, honey, and pounded fig roots. Another was to feed a pearl to a rooster. When the cock was killed, the pearl found inside it would be a milky white.

produced soft blankets, sheets, and clothing.

Light and soft linen was perfect for the hot, dry Egyptian climate. Since they didn't absorb dye well, linen clothes were a golden or off-white color. Fabrics made from cotton and wool could be dyed.

## Paints, Dyes, and Makeup

Many papyrus documents listed recipes for making dyes from plants and minerals. One of the most popular colors was royal purple. This color could be made by boiling algae or lichens together with ground alum. There were also recipes for reds, pinks, yellows, greens, and blues.

Color was ever-present in Egyptian society. Many surfaces—from the insides of tombs and pyramids to the walls and floors of houses—were painted in bright hues. Minerals, such as deep blue lapis lazuli or deep green malachite, were crushed into pigments and then mixed with water

**Sacred objects found in the tomb of an Egyptian woman include small pots for ointments and salves that were made with plants and minerals, a knife for preparing food, a mirror, and bowls for mixing dyes. Natural dyes were made from plant leaves and roots.**

to make paint. In building the tombs at the Valley of the Kings, stonecutters hewed chambers out of the rock. Then, plasterers whitewashed the walls and painters created vivid frescos upon them.

Makeup was similar to paint. Crushed pigments of copper ore made green eye shadow that was a sign of fertility. Lead ore created a darker gray-black shade of eye makeup. Various red pigments were made from ochres and iron oxide and then mixed with animal fat before being smeared on lips and cheeks. Makeup jars, tubes, and applicators were all popular accessories as were copper or bronze tweezers, polished mirrors, and hair curling tongs. In ancient Egypt, both men and women wore makeup.

Artists were highly respected members of society. Their important duties included illustrating sacred texts and painting the portraits of pharaohs on tombs and coffins. They carried out such tasks using a combination of techniques and talent that is still viewed as impressive even in present times.

Fortunately, subsequent generations recognized the value of these works and succeeded in preserving some of them. The surviving examples provide precious information about one of the world's oldest and richest civilizations. The Egyptian civilization is responsible for many of the advanced techniques and technologies that have become essential parts of our daily lives.

# TIMELINE

**5000–3100 BC**  (Early Predynastic Period) People begin farming along the banks of the Nile, growing wheat and barley and raising cattle.

Earliest irrigation systems are developed.

Copper mining and creation of copper tools begins.

**3100–2950 BC**  (Late Predynastic Period) King Menes creates the Egyptian state.

Earliest known hieroglyphic writing occurs.

Egyptians begin manufacturing papyrus.

Earliest glassmaking technology begins.

Looms are used to weave flax into linen.

**2950–2613 BC**  (First–Third Dynasties) Ancient capital of Memphis is founded.

First pyramid is built (King Djoser's Step Pyramid at Saqqâra).

Farmers are already using plows.

**2613–2495 BC**  (Fourth Dynasty) King Snefru orders the building of the first pyramid with sloping sides.

King Khufu's Great Pyramid at Giza is completed.

Sphinx is carved as the entrance to the pyramid of King Khafre.

**2495–2160 BC**  (Fifth–Eighth Dynasties) Reservoir at Fayum is built and is linked to the Nile by a canal.

*(continued on following page)*

# TIMELINE (continued from previous page)

**2160–1985 BC** (Ninth–Eleventh Dynasties) Scribes begin to use desks for writing.

Men begin using oxen to plow fields rather than doing the back-breaking work themselves.

**1985–1640 BC** (Twelfth–Fourteenth Dynasties) Metal fishing hooks come into use, replacing hooks made of bone.

**1640–1550 BC** (Fifteenth–Seventeenth Dynasties) Egyptian version of the chariot is invented.

Egyptians invent the shadoof to transport water.

**1550–1069 BC** (Eighteenth–Twentieth Dynasties) Elaborate tombs are built in the Valley of the Kings.

King Tutankhamen reigns briefly.

Ramses II builds the Temple at Abu Simbel. He rules Egypt for sixty-seven years and builds more monuments and erects more statues than any other pharaoh.

**1069–715 BC** (Twenty-first–Twenty-fourth Dynasties) Iron replaces copper in the making of many tools.

Almost all pyramids and tombs have been robbed of their treasures.

Camels are tamed and used for transportation.

**715–332 BC** (Twenty-fifth–Thirtieth Dynasties) Demotic Egyptian becomes the most common written script.

# GLOSSARY

**algae** A primitive type of aquatic plant.

**anesthetic** A drug, administered for medical or surgical purposes, that induces partial or total loss of sensation.

**cataracts** A clouding of the eye's lens.

**cuneiform** A type of ancient writing that uses small wedge-shaped characters.

**decan** One of the thirty-six star configurations identified by the Egyptians.

**dehydrate** To remove water.

**dike** A ditch or channel for water.

**dunghills** Mounds of animal excrement.

**embalming** Preventing a dead body from rotting by using chemicals, salts, and oils to preserve it.

**fertile** Fruitful, productive, and rich in material required for plant growth.

**fresco** A technique in painting in which pigment (color) is applied to wet plaster.

**harpoon** A spearlike weapon used in hunting and fishing.

**irrigation** Providing water to dry land (using canals, dikes, etc.).

**lichen** An algae and fungus growing together in a crustlike formation on rocks or tree trunks.

**lotus** A water lily that was a sacred Egyptian flower.

**negligence** Carelessness; a lack of concern.

**Nubian wild ass** African wild donkey.

**parchment** An ancient form of paper made from the skin of a sheep or goat.

**pigments** Dry powdery substances of pure color ground from minerals, metals, or plants.

**precursor** A forerunner; one that precedes and announces someone or something else.

**recede** To withdraw, retreat, drain away.

**reservoir** A natural or artificial pond or lake used for storing water.

**silt** Fine sediment that is usually a mixture of clay and sand.

**solder** To join or bond (usually two metals).

**Sumerians** An ancient people who established a nation of city-states in Sumer (today's Middle East) in the fourth millennium BC.

**till** To prepare earth for planting crops.

**tomb** A grave or other place of burial, such as a vault or chamber.

**wedge** A piece of metal or wood—thick at one edge and thin at the other—that acts as a lever when inserted into a narrow space.

# FOR MORE INFORMATION

## In Canada

Embassy of the Arab Republic of Egypt
454 Laurier Avenue East
Ottawa, ON K1N 6R3
e-mail: egyptemb@sympatico.ca
Web site: http://www.egyptembassy.ca

Royal Ontario Museum
100 Queen's Park
Toronto, ON M5S 2C6
e-mail: info@rom.on.ca
Web site: http://www.rom.on.ca/egypt/
case/about

## In the United Kingdom

The British Museum
Department of Ancient Egypt and Sudan
Great Russell Street
London, United Kingdom WC1B 3DG
e-mail: information@
thebritishmuseum.ac.uk
Web site: http://www.thebritishmuseum.
ac.uk/aes/aeshome.html

## In the United States

Embassy of the Arab Republic of Egypt
3521 International Court NW
Washington, DC 20008
e-mail: embassy@egyptembdc.org
Web site: http://www.egyptembassy.us

The Metropolitan Museum of Art
1000 Fifth Avenue
New York, NY 10028
(212) 535-7710
Web site: http://www.metmuseum.org/
Works_of_Art/department.asp?dep=10

## Web Sites

Due to the changing nature of Internet
links, the Rosen Publishing Group, Inc.,
has developed an online list of Web
sites related to the subject of this book.
This site is updated regularly. Please use
this link to access this list:

http://www.rosenlinks.com/taw/teae

# FOR FURTHER READING

Balkwill, Richard. *Clothes and Crafts in Ancient Egypt*. Milwaukee, WI: Gareth Stevens, 2000.

Berger, Melvin. *Baboons Waited on Tables in Ancient Egypt!: Weird Facts About Ancient Civilizations*. New York, NY: Scholastic, 1997.

Croshcr, Judith. *Technology in the Time of Ancient Egypt*. Austin, TX: Raintree/Steck-Vaughn, 1998.

Defrates, Joanna. *What Do We Know About the Egyptians?* New York, NY: Peter Bedrick Books, 1991.

Morley, Jacqueline. *How Would You Survive as an Ancient Egyptian?* New York, NY: Franklin Watts, 1996.

Stanley, Diane, and Peter Vennema. *Cleopatra*. New York, NY: Morrow Junior Books, 1994.

# BIBLIOGRAPHY

Baines, John, and Jaromír Malék. *Atlas of Ancient Egypt*. Oxford, UK: Phaidon, 1980.

Brier, Bob. *Ancient Egyptian Magic*. New York, NY: Quill Press, 1981.

The British Museum. "Ancient Egypt." Retrieved April 2005 (http://www.ancientegypt.co.uk/menu.html).

Egypt State Information Service. "Life of Ancient Egyptians." Retrieved April 2005 (http://www.sis.gov.eg/pharo/html/front.htm).

Hart, George. *Ancient Egypt*. Rev. ed. New York, NY: DK Publishing, 2004.

Kinnaer, Jacques. "The Ancient Egypt Site." Retrieved April 2005 (http://www.ancient-egypt.org).

Thinkquest. "Technology of Ancient Egypt." Retrieved April 2005 (http://library.thinkquest.org/J002046F/technology.htm).

Tour Egypt. "Egypt Antiquities and Ancient Egypt." Retrieved April 2005 (http://touregypt.net/egyptantiquities).

# INDEX

## About the Author

Canadian professor M. Solodky has a business degree from Northwestern University in Chicago. In the 1970s and '80s, he spent some time in several African nations, including Egypt, on behalf of CIDA, the Canadian International Development Agency. While helping to develop business programs at African universities, Professor Solodky also cultivated a deep interest in the diverse cultures and artistic traditions of the northern and eastern regions of Africa. Among the many cultures that fascinated him was that of ancient Egypt.

## Photo Credits

Cover Erich Lessing/Art Resource, NY; cover inset © The British Museum/ HIP/The Image Works; p. 4 Library of Congress Prints and Photograph Division; p. 6 Library of Congress Geography and Map Division; p. 8 The Art Archive/Dagli Orti; p. 9 Erich Lessing Art Resource, NY; p. 10 Erich Lessing/Art Resource, NY; p. 11 Erich Lessing/Art Resource, NY; p. 14 Erich Lessing/Art Resource, NY; p. 15 © The British Library/HIP/Art Resource, NY; p. 16 The Art Archive/ Dagli Orti; p. 19 The Art Archive/ Pharaonic Village Cairo/Dagli Orti; p. 22 Werner Forman/Art Resource, NY; p. 24 © Roger Wood/Corbis; p. 25 Valley of the Kings, Thebes, Egypt/ Bridgeman Art Library; p. 26 Library of Congress Prints and Photograph Division; p. 29 © Brooklyn Museum of Art, New York, USA, Charles Edwin Wilbour Fund/ Bridgeman Art Library; p. 30 Scala/Art Resource, NY; p. 31 © The British Museum/HIP/Art Resource, NY; p. 35 Werner Forman/Art Resource, NY; p. 36 The Art Archive/Egyptian Museum Cairo/Dagli Orti; p. 39 Fitzwilliam Museum, University of Cambridge, UK/Bridgeman Art Library.

**Editor**: Annie Sommers
**Designer**: Evelyn Horovicz
**Photo Researcher**: Jeff Wendt